PAPERBACK **PLUS**

Contents

About the Author

Carla Stevens always felt a sense of great adventure while riding on the cane seats of the Third Avenue Elevated when she was a child. Intrigued by an article about the stranded El trains during the 1888 blizzard, she wrote this story. Ms. Stevens was born in New York City and now lives in Bridgewater, Connecticut. She is a faculty member at the New School in New York City where she conducts writing workshops. This is her seventh book.

About the Artist

Margot Tomes has ancestors who came to New York in the 1820s, and she can remember hearing her grandparents tell stories of The Great Blizzard of 1888. Born in Yonkers, New York, Ms. Tomes grew up on Long Island and now lives in New York City. She studied art at Pratt Institute, and has illustrated more than forty books for children.

Anna, Grandpa, and the Big Storm

The snow was blowing sideways, pricking Anna's face like sharp needles. "Maybe we should go back home, Grandpa," Anna said. "I don't care so much any more about that spelling bee."

"Of course you care, Anna," said Grandpa. "And I'm going to see that you get to school."

Later, when Anna and Grandpa are trapped in a car on the Third Avenue elevated train, all thoughts of school and spelling bees are forgotten. They're afraid they may never get home again. What happens to Anna and Grandpa and the other snowbound passengers makes a warm and exciting adventure story based on an actual historical event.

In a gentle, easy-to-read style, Carla Stevens portrays the sensitive relationship between a young girl and her determined grandfather. Margot Tomes's lively illustrations transport the reader back in time to The Great Blizzard of 1888.

Anna, Grandpa, and the Big Storm

ANNA, GRANDPA, and the BIG STORM

Carla Stevens

pictures by
Margot Tomes

HOUGHTON MIFFLIN COMPANY
BOSTON
ATLANTA   DALLAS   GENEVA, ILLINOIS   PALO ALTO   PRINCETON

For Marie—C.S.

Acknowledgments

For each of the selections listed below, grateful acknowledgment is made for permission to excerpt and/or reprint original or copyrighted materials, as follows:

Selections

Anna, Grandpa, and the Big Storm, by Carla Stevens, illustrated by Margot Tomes. Text copyright © 1982 by Carla Stevens. Illustrations copyright © 1982 by Margot Tomes. Reprinted by permission of Clarion Books, a division of Houghton Mifflin Company. All rights reserved.

"The Blizzard Men," by Alice M. Sayer. Every attempt has been made to locate the rightsholder of this work. If the rightsholder should read this, please contact Houghton Mifflin Company, School Permissions, 222 Berkeley Street, Boston, MA 02116-3764.

"What is A Blizzard?" from *Blizzards,* by Steven Otfinoski. Copyright © 1994 by Blackbirch Graphics, Inc. Reprinted by permission of Twenty-First Century Books, a division of Henry Holt and Company.

Photography

ii Courtesy of Carla Stevens. **60–61** New York Historical Society. **62** The Bettmann Archive (t); Brown Brothers (b). **63** New York Historical Society. **64** Museum of the City of New York. **65** Museum of the City of New York. **66** New York Historical Society. **67** Museum of the City of New York.

1997 Impression
Houghton Mifflin Edition, 1996
Copyright © 1996 by Houghton Mifflin Company. All rights reserved.

Printed in the U.S.A.

ISBN: 0-395-73231-X

789-B-99 98 97

Contents

❋ 1 ❋

Grandpa Comes to Visit

Anna sat at the kitchen table trying to study her spelling words. But it was no use. Grandpa was making a fuss again.

"I want to go home," he said.

"You have been here only three days," Anna's father replied. "I will take you home next Saturday."

"I can't wait that long," said Grandpa.

Mrs. Romano looked at her father sternly. "Now see here, Papa. Next time when we invite you, you can say 'no.' But this time you said 'yes.' And that's why you are here."

Grandpa frowned. "There's nothing for me

to do in the city," he said. "Especially on a rainy day."

"Don't you like us, Grandpa?" Tony asked.

Grandpa Jensen looked down at his young grandson. "Of course I do, Tony. I just can't stand being cooped up like a rooster."

Anna pushed her chair back and stood up. How could she get her homework done with Grandpa fussing and stewing all week? She walked to the front parlor and looked out of the window onto Fifteenth Street. Not even the halos of light cast by the gas lamps could brighten this dreary Sunday.

Grandpa came and stood behind her. "Past time for milking. Never thought I'd miss the farm so," he said softly.

For a moment Anna felt sorry for her grandfather. But then he started grumbling again. "How a man can live in a city like this is more than I can understand."

Later, when Anna was in bed, Mama came to kiss her goodnight. "Grandpa fusses a lot," Anna whispered.

"I know," said her mother. "I invited Grandpa to visit us. I thought it would be a change for him after your grandmother died."

"He isn't polite," Anna said.

Anna's mother smiled. "Your grandfather has always said just what he thinks."

Anna sighed. "Still I wished he liked it better here."

"You must try to make him feel at home, Anna. He's an old man."

"Yes, Mama."

"Now go to sleep." Mama kissed her on the forehead. She closed the door quietly behind her.

Anna tried to think what she could do to make Grandpa feel more at home. She and Tony could take him for a walk to Washington Square Park. They could show him the gray squirrel's nest in the big oak tree near the arch, and the daffodils already in bloom around the fountain.

Anna listened to the sleet hitting the skylight above her head. "Oh, I hope tomorrow will be a nice day," she thought just before she fell asleep.

✾ 2 ✾

Snow in the Morning

When Anna woke up she thought it was still night. No light came through the skylight. She turned on her side in bed and looked through the doorway into the kitchen. Tony was at the table eating his oatmeal. Grandpa was pouring a bucket of coal into the big stove.

Anna jumped out of bed and ran into the kitchen to get dressed. Mama came in from the parlor.

"What time is it, Mama?" Anna asked, warming her hands over the hot stove.

"Almost seven thirty," Mama said. "Go to

the front window and see what is happening outside."

Anna looked out of the window. It was snowing so hard, she could scarcely see the houses across the street.

"Don't worry, it won't last," Grandpa said. "After all, it's almost the middle of March."

Mama put a bowl of hot oatmeal on the table for Anna. "Maybe you should stay home from school today," she said.

"I can't, Mama. Today is the last day of the spelling bee. If I win, I'll be in the City Finals."

Mrs. Romano sighed. "If Papa were here, he could take you."

"Where is Papa?" Anna asked.

"He left very early to take his new harnesses to the trolley car station in Harlem."

"What's the matter with me?" Grandpa asked. "Why can't I take her? Besides, I want to stop at Mr. Knudsen's shop and get more tobacco."

"But I want to walk to school by myself, the way I always do," Anna said.

Grandpa gave Anna a sad look. "It's no fun when you're old." He shook his head. "No one thinks you're good for much of anything."

"I don't think that, Grandpa," Anna said quickly.

"But it's snowing hard out, Papa," Anna's mother said.

"Do you think I've never seen snow before?" Grandpa asked. "Anna's going to school, and I'm going to take her. And that's that!"

"All right, all right, go along you two,"

Mama said. "But take the El, Anna. Then you won't have to walk those eight blocks."

Grandpa put on his overcoat and his hat with ear flaps and his big galoshes.

"And be sure to come right back if school is closed," Anna's mother added.

"We will," Anna said. "Good-bye, Mama. Good-bye, Tony."

"Come on, Anna," Grandpa said cheerfully. "Let's see what your city looks like in the snow!"

❊3❊

Out with Grandpa

As soon as Anna started down the front steps, she knew something was different about this snow. It was not falling down. It was blowing sideways, pricking her face like sharp needles. She pulled her muffler up over her nose.

Anna and Grandpa plodded down the street. The wind whipped the snow in great swirls around them as they crossed Broadway and tramped through Union Square. When they reached the firehouse, Anna saw a fireman shoveling snow away from the stable doors.

"Morning!" Grandpa said brightly. "Quite a storm for this time of year!"

"It caught us by surprise," the fireman replied. "Where are you going on a day like this?"

"To school," Grandpa said. "My granddaughter, Anna, is in the spelling bee finals."

"Good luck to you, little lassie," the fireman said.

Anna pulled her muffler down from her mouth so she could say "thank you." But she felt embarrassed. She didn't like it when Grandpa talked about her to strangers.

They finally reached the corner of Fifteenth Street and Third Avenue. Grandpa turned the door handle of Mr. Knudsen's tobacco shop. But the door wouldn't open.

Anna cleared a spot on the window with her mitten and peered inside. It was dark.

"What kind of shopkeeper is he?" Grandpa
grumbled. "He doesn't even come to work!"

"But Grandpa, it's snowing hard now."

"Child, do you think the world stands still
every time it snows?" Grandpa looked at her
crossly.

It seemed to be growing colder by the minute. The snow, blown by the wind, was beginning to drift along the north side of the street. Only a few people were making their way up Third Avenue.

"Maybe we should go back home, Grandpa," Anna said. "I don't care so much any more about that spelling bee."

"Of course you care, Anna! And I'm going to see that you get to school."

"But Grandpa, the wind is getting so strong I can hardly walk." Anna tried not to sound frightened.

"You don't have to walk. We'll do just what your mother suggested. We'll ride the Elevated."

Anna looked up. It was snowing so hard that she could barely see the train tracks of the Third Avenue El above her.

❊ 4 ❊

The Third Avenue El

Anna followed Grandpa up the long flight of steps to the Fourteenth Street El station. No one was at the ticket booth so they ducked under the turnstile to the platform. They stood out of the wind at the head of the stairs. Anna could see only one other person waiting for a train on the uptown side.

Anna looked at her rosy-cheeked grandfather. Snow clung to his moustache and eyebrows and froze. They looked like tiny icebergs.

"Here comes the train!" Grandpa shouted.

A steam engine, pulling two green cars,

puffed toward them. When the train stopped, Anna and Grandpa hurried across the platform and stepped inside. There were lots of empty seats. They sat down behind a large woman. She took up most of the seat in front of them.

Anna pulled off her hat. Her pom-pom looked like a big white snowball. She shook it, spraying the floor with wet snow. The conductor came up the aisle and stopped at their seat.

Grandpa said, "No one was at the station to sell us a ticket."

"That will be five cents," the conductor said. "Each."

"You mean I have to pay for her, too?" Grandpa's eyes twinkled.

"Grandpa," Anna whispered, tugging at his arm. "I'm almost eight years old."

Grandpa and the conductor laughed. Anna
didn't like to be teased. She turned away and
tried to look out, but snow covered the windows.

Grandpa leaned forward. "Quite a storm,"
he said to the woman in the seat in front of
them. "Nothing like the Blizzard of '72,
though. Why it was so cold, the smoke froze
as it came out of the chimney!"

There he goes again, Anna thought. Why does Grandpa always talk to strangers?

A woman holding a basket sat across from them. She leaned over. "In Poland, when I was a little girl, it snowed like this all winter long."

The woman in the seat ahead turned around. "This storm can't last. First day of spring is less than two weeks away."

"That's just what I was telling my daughter this morning!" Grandpa said.

Anna could see that Grandpa was growing more cheerful by the minute.

Suddenly the train stopped.

"What's the trouble?" the woman from Poland asked. "Conductor, why has the train stopped?"

The conductor didn't reply. He opened the car door and stepped out onto the platform. No one inside said a word.

Then Grandpa stood up. "I'll find out what's the matter."

Anna tugged at his coat sleeve. "Oh, please sit down, Grandpa." He didn't seem to understand how scared she felt. How she wished she had stayed home!

The door opened again and the conductor entered the car. He was covered with snow.

"We're stuck," he said. "The engine can't move. Too much snow has drifted onto the tracks ahead. We'll have to stay here until help comes."

"Did you hear that, Anna?" Grandpa almost bounced up and down in his seat. "We're stuck! Stuck and stranded on the Third Avenue El! What do you think about that!"

✳5✳

Stranded

When Anna heard the news, she grew even more frightened. "Mama will be so worried. She doesn't know where we are."

"She knows you are with me," Grandpa said cheerfully. "That's all she needs to know." He leaned forward again. "We might as well get acquainted," he said. "My name is Erik Jensen, and this is my granddaughter, Anna."

The woman in the seat ahead turned around. "Josie Sweeney," she said. "Pleased to meet you."

"How-dee-do," said the woman across the

aisle. "I'm Mrs. Esther Polanski. And this is my friend, Miss Ruth Cohen."

Someone tapped Anna on her shoulder. She turned around. Two young men smiled.

One man said, "John King and my brother, Bruce."

A young woman with a high fur collar and a big hat sat by herself at the rear of the car. Anna looked in her direction. "My name is Anna Romano," she said shyly. "I'm Addie

Beaver," said the young woman. She smiled and wrapped her coat more tightly around her.

It was growing colder and colder inside the car. When the conductor shook the snow off his clothes, it no longer melted into puddles on the floor.

"We'll all freeze to death if we stay here," moaned Mrs. Sweeney.

"Oooooo, my feet are so cold," Addie Beaver said.

Anna looked at her high-button shoes and felt sorry for Addie Beaver. Even though Anna had on her warm boots, her toes began to grow cold, too. She stood in the aisle and stamped her feet up and down.

Suddenly Anna had an idea. "Grandpa!" she said. "I know a game we can play that might help keep us warm."

"Why Anna, what a good idea," Grandpa replied.

"It's called, 'Simon Says'."

"Listen everybody!" Grandpa shouted. "My granddaughter, Anna, knows a game that will help us stay warm."

"How do we play, Anna?" asked Mrs. Polanski. "Tell us."

"Everybody has to stand up," said Anna.

"Come on, everybody," Grandpa said. "We must keep moving if we don't want to freeze to death."

Miss Beaver was the first to stand. Then John and Bruce King stood up. Grandpa bowed first to Mrs. Sweeney, then to Mrs. Polanski and Miss Cohen. "May I help you, ladies?" he asked. They giggled and stood up. Now everybody was looking at Anna.

"All right," she said. "You must do only what Simon tells you to do. If *I* tell you to do something, you mustn't do it."

"I don't understand," Mrs. Sweeney said.

"Maybe we'll catch on if we start playing," Grandpa said.

"All right," Anna said. "I'll begin. Simon says, 'Clap your hands'."

Everybody began to clap hands.

"Simon says, 'Stop'!"

NEW YORK ELEVA

Everybody stopped.

"Good!" Anna said. "Simon says, 'Follow me'!" Anna marched down the aisle of the car, then around one of the poles, then back again. Everyone followed her.

"Simon says, 'Stop'!"

Everyone stopped.

Anna patted her head and rubbed her stomach at the same time.

"Simon says, 'Pat your head and rub your stomach.' Like this."

Everyone began to laugh at one another.

"Simon says, 'Swing your arms around and around'."

"Ooof! This is hard work!" puffed Mrs. Sweeney.

"Now. Touch your toes!"

Mrs. Sweeney bent down and tried to touch her toes.

"Oh! Oh! You're out, Mrs. Sweeney!" Anna said.

"Why am I out?" She asked indignantly.

Anna giggled. "Because *Simon* didn't say to touch your toes. *I* did!"

Mrs. Sweeney sat down. "It's just as well," she panted. "I was getting all tired out."

"Is everyone warming up?" Grandpa asked.

"Yes! Yes!" they all shouted.

Snow was sifting like flour through the cracks around the windows. Just then, the door opened. A blast of icy cold air blew into the car. Everyone shivered. It was the conductor coming back in again.

"Get ready to leave," he said. "The firemen are coming!"

❋6❋

Firemen to the Rescue

Everyone rushed to the door and tried to look out. The snow stung Anna's eyes. The wind almost took her breath away.

The conductor closed the door again quickly. "The wind is so fierce it's going to be hard to get a ladder up this high. We're at least thirty feet above Third Avenue."

Ladder! Thirty feet! Anna shivered.

"Oh, Lord help me," groaned Mrs. Sweeney. "I'll never be able to climb down a ladder." She gave Grandpa a pleading look.

"Oh, yes you will, Mrs. Sweeney," he said.

"Once you get the hang of it, it's easy."

"In all that wind?" Mrs. Sweeney said. "Never!"

"Don't worry, Mrs. Sweeney. You won't blow away," said Grandpa.

Anna looked at Grandpa. "I'm scared too," she said.

"And what about me?" asked Mrs. Polanski. "I can't stand heights."

The door opened and a fireman appeared.

He shook the snow off his clothes. "We'll take you down one at a time. Who wants to go first?"

No one spoke.

"Anna," said Grandpa. "You're a brave girl. You go first."

"I'm afraid to climb down the ladder, Grandpa."

"Why Anna, I'm surprised at you. Don't you remember how you climbed down from the hayloft last summer? It was easy."

"You can do it, Anna," said Miss Cohen.

"Pretend we're still playing that game. Simon says, 'Go down the ladder'," said Mrs. Sweeney.

"So go now," Miss Cohen said. "We'll see you below."

"I'll be right below you to shield you from the wind. You won't fall," said the fireman.

Anna shook with fear. She didn't want to
be first to go down the ladder. But how could
she disappoint the others?

Grandpa opened the door. The conductor
held her hand. Anna put first one foot, then
the other, on the ladder. The fierce wind
pulled her and pushed her. Icy snow stuck to
her clothes, weighing her down.

The fireman was below her on the ladder. His strong arms were around her, holding her steady. With her left foot, Anna felt for the rung below.

Step by step by step, she cautiously went down the ladder. Thirty steps. Would she never reach bottom? One foot plunged into snow and then the other. Oh, so much snow! It covered her legs and reached almost to her waist.

"Stay close to the engine until the rest are down," the fireman said.

Anna struggled through the deep snow to the fire engine. The horses, whipped by the icy wind and snow, stood still, their heads low. Anna huddled against the side of the engine. The roar of the storm was growing louder.

❋ 7 ❋

The Storm Grows Worse

First came Mrs. Polanski, then Ruth Cohen. Then Bruce and John King. Then Addie Beaver. One at a time, the fireman helped each person down the ladder. Now only Grandpa and Mrs. Sweeney remained to be rescued.

Anna could see two shapes on the ladder, one behind the other. The fireman was bringing down someone else.

"Oh, I hope it's Grandpa," Anna said to Addie Beaver.

Suddenly she gasped. She could hardly believe her eyes. One minute the two shapes were there. The next minute they weren't!

Everyone struggled through the deep snow to find out who had fallen off the ladder.

Anna was first to reach the fireman who was brushing snow off his clothes. "What happened?" she asked.

"Mrs. Sweeney missed a step on the ladder. Down she went, taking me with her," the fireman replied.

Mrs. Sweeney lay sprawled in the snow nearby. Her arms and legs were spread out, as if she were going to make a snow angel.

"Are you all right, Mrs. Sweeney?" Grandpa asked. Anna had not seen Grandpa come down the ladder by himself. Now he stood beside her.

"I'm just fine, Mr. Jensen. I think I'm going to lie right here until the storm is over."

"Oh no you're not!" Grandpa said. He and

a fireman each took one of Mrs. Sweeney's arms. They pulled her to her feet.

Anna couldn't help giggling. Now Mrs. Sweeney looked like a giant snow lady!

"Climb onto the engine," said a fireman.

"We must get the horses back to the firehouse. The temperature is dropping fast."

"We live only two blocks from here," Mrs. Polanski and Miss Cohen said. "We're going to try to get home."

"We'll see that you get there," John King said. "We live on Lafayette Street." The young men and the two ladies linked arms and trudged off through the snow.

"What about you, Miss Beaver?" Grandpa asked. She looked confused.

"Hey, this is no tea party! Let's go!" said the fireman.

"You come with us then, Miss Beaver," Grandpa said. "You too, Mrs. Sweeney."

Anna's fingers were numb with cold. She could hardly hold onto the railing of the engine. Often she had seen the horses racing down the street to a fire. Now they plodded along very, very slowly through the deep snow.

No one spoke. The wind roared and shrieked. The snow blinded them. One fireman jumped off the engine and tried to lead the horses forward.

Anna huddled against the side of the engine, hiding her face in her arms. It was taking them forever to reach the firehouse.

Just then, the horses turned abruptly to the left. The next moment they were inside the stable, snorting and stamping their hooves.

Several men ran forward to unhitch the engine. Everyone began brushing the icy snow off their clothes.

Suddenly Grandpa became very serious. "The thermometer says five degrees above zero, and the temperature is still dropping.

We must get home as fast as possible. Mrs. Sweeney, you and Miss Beaver had better come with us."

"Here, Miss," a fireman said. "Put these boots on. You can return them when the storm is over."

"Oh, thank you," Addie Beaver said.

Anna had forgotten about Addie's high-button shoes.

"Whatever you do, Anna, you are *not* to let go of my hand." Grandpa spoke firmly.

"Mr. Jensen, would you mind if I held your other hand?" asked Mrs. Sweeney.

"Not a bit," said Grandpa. "Anna, you take hold of Miss Beaver's hand. No one is to let go under *any* circumstances. Do you all understand?"

Anna had never heard Grandpa talk like that before. Was he frightened too?

They plunged into the deep snow, moving
slowly along the south side of Fifteenth
Street. The wind had piled the snow into
huge drifts on the north side of the street.

When they reached Broadway, the wind was blowing up the avenue with the force of a hurricane. Telephone and telegraph wires were down. Thousands of them cut through the air like whips. If only they could reach the other side, Anna thought. Then they would be on their very own block.

No one spoke. They clung to one another as they blindly made their way across the avenue. Mrs. Sweeney lost her balance and fell forward in the snow. For a moment Anna thought she was there to stay. But Grandpa tugged at her arm and helped her get to her feet.

They continued on until they reached the other side. Now to find their house. How

lucky they were to live on the south side of the block. The snow had reached as high as the first-floor windows of the houses on the north side. At last they came to Number 44. Up the seven steps they climbed. Then through the front door and up more stairs. A moment later, Mr. Romano opened their apartment door. "Papa, you're home," Anna cried, and fell into her father's arms.

❋8❋

Home at Last!

Several hours later, Anna sat in the kitchen watching a checkers game. Mrs. Sweeney, wearing Grandpa's bathrobe, was playing checkers with Grandpa, while Miss Beaver, in Mama's clothes, chatted with Mama. Outside, the storm whistled and roared. Tomorrow would be time enough to study her spelling, Anna decided. Now she just wanted to enjoy the company.

Suddenly Grandpa pushed his chair back. "You win, Mrs. Sweeney. Where did you learn to play checkers?"

"I belong to a club," Mrs. Sweeney replied.

"I'm the champ. We meet every Tuesday. Maybe you will come with me next Tuesday, Mr. Jensen?"

"Why, I'd like that," answered Grandpa.

"You can't, Grandpa," Tony said. "You're going home Saturday."

"Who says so?" Grandpa asked.

"You did. Don't you remember?"

"Hush, Tony," Anna said. "Maybe he will stay a little longer. I think Grandpa likes the city better now."

Mrs. Romano smiled. "It took a snowstorm to change his mind."

"You call this a snowstorm?" said Grandpa. He winked at Anna. "When you are an old lady, Anna, as old as I am now, you will be telling your grandchildren all about our adventure in The Great Blizzard of 1888!"

The Great Blizzard of 1888

There really *was* a great blizzard in 1888. It began to snow early Monday morning, March 12th. Before the snow stopped on Tuesday, four to five feet had fallen in New York City. Seventy inches fell in Boston and in other parts of the east.

The winds blew at 75 miles an hour and piled the snow in huge drifts. Everywhere, people were stranded. In New York City, about 15,000 people were trapped in Elevated trains. Like Anna and Grandpa, they had to be rescued by firemen with ladders.

By Thursday of that same week, the sun was out again. The snow began to melt. Anna went to school and won the spelling bee. And Grandpa walked down to Sullivan Street to play checkers again with Josie Sweeney.

SPECIAL SNOW SHEET.

NO. 1,926.

Morning

NEW YORK, TUESI

BLIZ

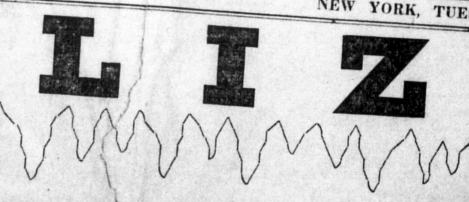

with the snow and wind, he was disconcerted at not finding his usual carriage coming along.

All the street-cars were stopped.

When all the horse-cars stop, New York is very near a revolution. But the citizen spoken of went a step further and found not only a revolution, but an earthquake.

He walked along—no means of riding being at hand—to an Elevated Railroad station and boarded a train to go "downtown."

Then he learned what a blizzard was.

The Elevated trains wouldn't run.

New York had been struck by the most terrible, the most unreasonable storm it has had for more than half a century, perhaps the most violent storms that ever came here, but the Signal Service clerk isn't old enough to remember, and nobody else has authority to speak.

Then the average citizen tried to get a cab.

There were cabs running up and down town. People who were unable to breast the storm and walk to business were unable to get to their stores and offices.

A Good Day for Cabbies.

But it cost them a good bit. A Hansom cab from Forty-second street to the Sub-Treasury building cost $10 before 12 o'clock. By the middle of the afternoon it cost $

A JOURNAL reporter offered a ha take him from Chatham square to the accident. Seventy-sixth stre laughed to scorn.

Newspaper Row Beats the Deck.
Nowhere else in New York

preferred it to remaining for they knew not how long in the crowded train.

Life and Limb Endangered.

Several times when the track ahead was full of pedestrians trains started, causing a panic among the imperilled people. But so far as learned no fatalities resulted from these occurrences.

As the noon hour approached and the severity of the storm rather increased than diminished the trains ran more slowly and were dispatched less frequently.

The Great Danger.

The snow packed so hard in between the two guard rails that run beside the iron rails that the engineers feared to run their trains.

The danger was that the wheels of the engine, perhaps of the cars, would run up on the snow. Then a train might topple over into the street. This is the one accident most dreaded by the Manhattan Company.

On Ladders from the Elevated.

A three-car train on Sixth avenue going down town was stopped at 8:30 a. m. in Third street, between Sixth avenue and South Fifth avenue.

And not only did it come to a stop, but it stayed stationary so long that there was scant hope among the passengers of any release till the storm should blow over.

Presently the Fire Department was called upon, and the nearest hook and ladder company coming to the rescue placed ladders against the Elevated road structure.

Before that some of the younger passengers had essayed to walk back to the

will tell. It was a journe but thousands had to m

Those who managed t safety yesterday, it is e the danger of a similar o

A HORSE-CA

Double and Triple Tea Ca

For the first time in s experienced a universa traffic. On every sur fac tie-up, while cabs, wagon of vehicles were sooner snow.

Before daylight every and every car started on reached City Hall. Mos doned en route, and even

THE SNOW TERROR.

New York Tied Up and Cut Off by Storm.

PARALYZED CITIES.

Cars, Trains, Business, Thea-

The New York *Morning Journal*
printed this special "icicle edition"
of the newspaper on March 13, 1888.

Journal.

ICICLE EDITION.

MARCH 13, 1888.

PRICE ONE CENT.

Z A ᴿᵀ D EXTRA

for driving a party of four two miles down town. The same driver charged a man $1 for the privilege of driving across Forty-second street from Third to Sixth avenue, the passenger sitting on top of a trunk and glad of the chance. A stable man had refused to turn out a hack for him up-

"Stalled" on Third Avenue.

der $25. Ten dollars to ride down town

anything toward setting them right until the blizzard passes away.

ALL WIRES ARE DOWN.

At 12 O'Clock a Complete Telegraphic Interruption is Announced.

At 12 o'clock last night the United Press sent out the following:

Since 7 p. m. we have had for part of the time communication with points in New York State and West to Chicago, and Chicago could reach Southern points; but we are now again cut off from all points. The wire we had was the only one working West out of New York. It was one of the old Baltimore & Ohio wires. It is now broken between Weehawken and Haverstraw, as well as all others by that route. The Western Union have no wires, nor the Postal. We have not had any Eastern point, nor Philadelphia, Baltimore nor Western

PANIC IN MID-AIR.

A Fatal Collision on the Third Avenue Elevated.

SNOW BLINDS THE ENGINEERS.

One Man Killed and Several Sustain Serious Injuries.

A heavily-loaded train pulled by two engines was slowly puffing southward over the snow-packed tracks of the Third Avenue "L" Road at 7 o'clock

Old New York

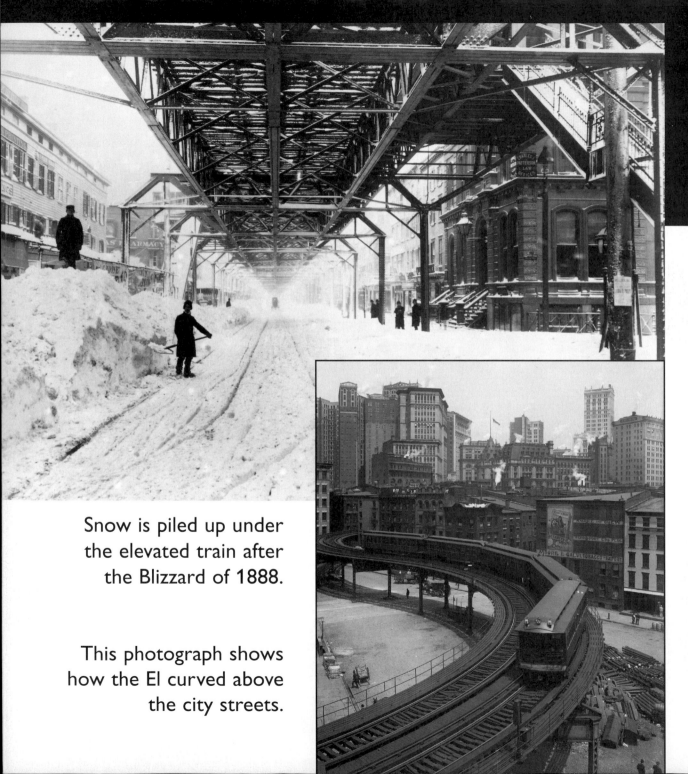

Snow is piled up under the elevated train after the Blizzard of 1888.

This photograph shows how the El curved above the city streets.

and the Blizzard of 1888

The El was not the only form of transportation to be shut down by the blizzard. This horsecar could not make it

A telephone pole on West 11th Street
was knocked down by the blizzard.

Mounds of snow
block the
entrance to
New York's
Exchange Court.

After the streets were shoveled, mountains of snow lined the sidewalks.

High winds knocked down signs and awnings throughout the city.

WHEN △ DISASTER △ STRIKES

BLIZZARDS

Steven Otfinoski

WHAT IS A
Blizzard?
by Steven Otfinoski

Blizzard—the very word sends a chill down the spine and brings to mind blinding snow and frigid temperatures. But just what makes a blizzard different from any other snowstorm? There are three main components to a blizzard—very cold temperatures, heavy snow, and most important of all, wind. Strong winds are what give a blizzard its tremendous power. Wind can drive snow so hard that visibility can be reduced to zero. It can sweep snow into monstrous drifts that can bury a car, or even an entire building.

The National Weather Service in Washington, D.C., defines a blizzard as any snowfall that is accompanied by sustained winds of 35 miles (56 kilometers) per hour or more, temperatures that fall as low as 10°F (-12°C), and visibility of less than 1,500 feet (458 meters). These conditions, the Weather Service reports, must persist for at least three hours to cause a snowstorm to turn into a blizzard. A severe blizzard has winds that are greater than 45 miles (72 kilometers) per hour, temperatures below 10°F (-12°C), and visibility approaching zero.

The Blizzard Men

by Alice M. Sayer

Come, Blizzard Men of Eighty-eight,
  Let's gather 'round and mark the date,
The Twelfth of March so long ago,
  When the snow came down and the winds did blow.
The storm ne'er ceased for three whole days,
  The clouds hid all the sun's bright rays,
No trains could run, all wires down,
  No contacts made with any town.

We arose that morn to a dazzling sight,
  The snow was piled in mounds so white,
We wondered how we'd get to work,
  For we are the kind who do not shirk.
We'll tell you tales of ice and sleet,
  And drifts of snow across the street;
The greatest storm we'll ever know,
  Which came to us so long ago.